The LITTLE RED ANT and the GREAT BIG CRUMB

▼▼▼▼▼▼▼▼ A Mexican Fable ▼▼▼▼▼▼▼▼

Retold by Shirley Climo
Illustrated by Francisco X. Mora

Clarion Books/New York

Clarion Books
a Houghton Mifflin Company imprint
215 Park Avenue South, New York, NY 10003
Text copyright © 1995 by Shirley Climo
Illustrations copyright © 1995 by Francisco X. Mora

The illustrations for this book were executed in watercolor on paper.
The text is set in 16/22-point Optima.

Printed in The USA

Library of Congress Cataloging-in-Publication Data

Climo, Shirley.
The little red ant and the great big crumb / by Shirley Climo ;
illustrated by Francisco X. Mora.
p.   cm.
Summary: A small red ant finds a crumb in a Mexican cornfield, but she
is afraid that she lacks the strength to move it herself and goes off to
find an animal that can.
ISBN 0-395-70732-3
[1. Ants—Fiction.   2. Animals—Fiction.   3. Self-esteem—Fiction.]
I. Mora, Francisco X., ill.   II. Title.
PZ7.C62247Li   1995
[E]—dc20   94-27073
CIP
AC

WOZ   10   9   8   7   6   5   4   3   2   1

For Nina, who read this story once
and was willing to read it twice
—S.C.

Para Sergito y Panchito con mucho cariñito
—F.M.

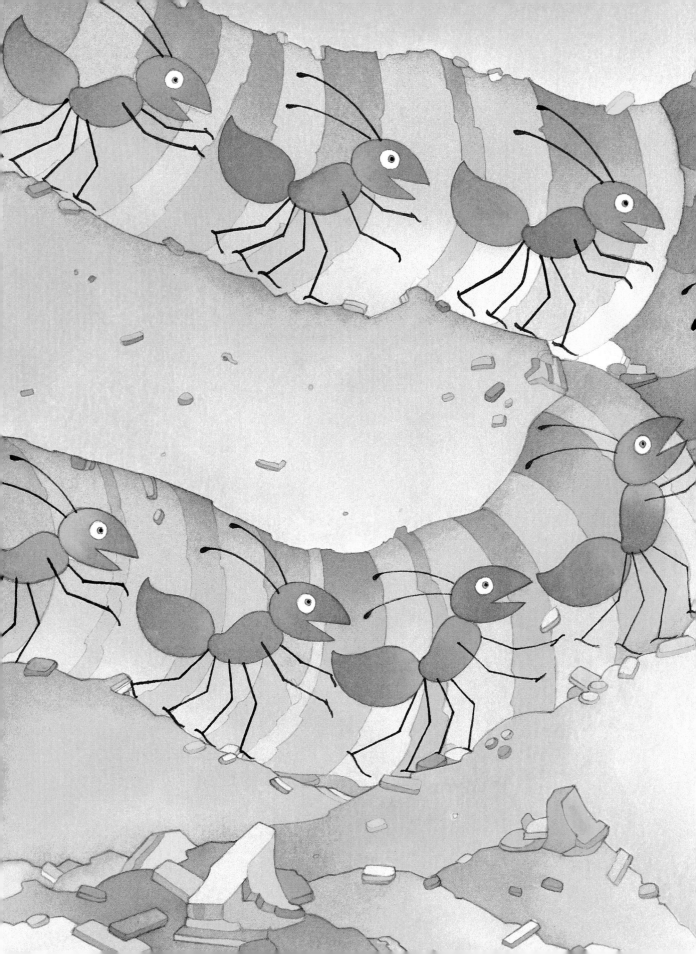

CHAPTER SUMMARY • CONSUMER PROTECTION—CONTINUED

Health and Safety Protection (See pages 561–564.)	1. *Food and drugs*—The Federal Food, Drug and Cosmetic Act of 1938, as amended, protects consumers against adulterated and misbranded foods and drugs. The act establishes food standards, specifies safe levels of potentially hazardous food additives, and sets classifications of food and food advertising.
	2. *Consumer product safety*—The Consumer Product Safety Act of 1972 seeks to protect consumers from risk of injury from hazardous products. The Consumer Product Safety Commission has the power to remove products that are deemed imminently hazardous from the market and to ban the manufacture and sale of hazardous products.
Credit Protection (See pages 564–569.)	1. *Consumer Credit Protection Act, Title I (Truth-in-Lending Act, or TILA)*—A disclosure law that requires sellers and lenders to disclose credit terms or loan terms in certain transactions, including retail and installment sales and loans, car loans, home-improvement loans, and certain real estate loans. Additionally, the TILA provides rules governing equal credit opportunity, credit-card protection, and consumer leases.
	2. *Fair Credit Reporting Act*—Entitles consumers to request verification of the accuracy of a credit report and to have unverified or false information removed from their files.
	3. *Fair Debt Collection Practices Act*—Prohibits debt collectors from using unfair debt-collection practices, such as contacting the debtor at his or her place of employment if the employer objects or at unreasonable times, contacting third parties about the debt, and harassing the debtor, for example.
State Consumer Protection Laws (See pages 569–571.)	State laws often provide for greater consumer protection against deceptive trade practices than do federal laws. In addition, the warranty and unconscionability provisions of the Uniform Commercial Code protect consumers against sellers' deceptive practices.

FOR REVIEW

Answers for the even-numbered questions in this For Review *section can be found in Appendix O at the end of this text.*

1. When will advertising be deemed deceptive?

2. What special rules apply to telephone solicitation?

3. What is Regulation Z, and to what type of transactions does it apply?

4. How does the Federal Food, Drug and Cosmetic Act protect consumers?

5. What are the major federal statutes providing for consumer protection in credit transactions?

QUESTIONS AND CASE PROBLEMS

17–1. Unsolicited Merchandise. Andrew, a California resident, received a flyer in the U.S. mail announcing a new line of regional cookbooks distributed by the Every-Kind Cookbook Co. Andrew was not interested and threw the flyer away. Two days later, Andrew received in the mail an introductory cookbook entitled *Lower Mongolian Regional Cookbook*, as announced in the flyer, on a "trial basis" from Every-Kind. Andrew was not interested but did not go to the trouble to return the cookbook. Every-Kind demanded payment of $20.95 for the *Lower Mongolian Regional Cookbook*. Discuss whether Andrew can be required to pay for the cookbook.

Question with Sample Answer

17–2. On June 28, a salesperson for Renowned Books called on the Gonchars at their home. After a very persuasive sales pitch by the agent, the Gonchars agreed in writing

to purchase a twenty-volume set of historical encyclopedias from Renowned Books for a total of $299. A down payment of $35 was required, with the remainder of the cost to be paid in monthly payments over a one-year period. Two days later the Gonchars, having second thoughts, contacted the book company and stated that they had decided to rescind the contract. Renowned Books said this would be impossible. Has Renowned Books violated any consumer law by not allowing the Gonchars to rescind their contract? Explain.

For a sample answer to this question, go to Appendix P at the end of this text.

17–3. Credit Protection. Maria Ochoa receives two new credit cards on May 1. She has solicited one of them from Midtown Department Store, and the other arrives unsolicited from High-Flying Airlines. During the month of May, Ochoa makes numerous credit-card purchases from Midtown

Department Store, but she does not use the High-Flying Airlines card. On May 31, a burglar breaks into Ochoa's home and steals both credit cards, along with other items. Ochoa notifies the Midtown Department Store of the theft on June 2, but she fails to notify High-Flying Airlines. Using the Midtown credit card, the burglar makes a $500 purchase on June 1 and a $200 purchase on June 3. The burglar then charges a vacation flight on the High-Flying Airlines card for $1,000 on June 5. Ochoa receives the bills for these charges and refuses to pay them. Discuss Ochoa's liability in these situations.

17–4. Deceptive Advertising. Kraft, Inc., produces individually wrapped cheese slices, called "Singles Slices," which are made from real cheese and which cost more than the imitation cheese slices on the market. In the early 1980s, Kraft began losing its market share to an increasing number of producers of imitation cheese slices. Kraft responded with a series of advertisements collectively known as the "Five Ounces of Milk" campaign. The ads claimed that Kraft Singles cost more than imitation slices because they were made from five ounces of milk rather than less expensive ingredients. The ads also implied that because each slice contained five ounces of milk, Kraft Singles contained a higher calcium content than imitation cheese slices. The Federal Trade Commission (FTC) filed a complaint against Kraft, charging that Kraft had materially misrepresented the calcium content and relative calcium benefit of Kraft Singles. Was Kraft's advertising campaign deceptive and likely to mislead consumers? [*Kraft, Inc. v. FTC*, 970 F.2d 311 (7th Cir. 1992)]

Case Problem with Sample Answer

17–5. CrossCheck, Inc., provides check-authorization services to retail merchants. When a customer presents a check, the merchant contacts CrossCheck, which estimates the probability that the check will clear the bank. If the check is within an acceptable statistical range, CrossCheck notifies the merchant. If the check is dishonored, the merchant sends it to CrossCheck, which pays it. CrossCheck then attempts to redeposit the check. If this fails, CrossCheck takes further steps to collect the amount. CrossCheck attempts to collect on more than two thousand checks per year and spends $2 million on these efforts, which involve about 7 percent of its employees and 6 percent of its total expenses. William Winterstein took his truck to C&P Auto Service Center, Inc., for a tune-up and paid for the service with a check. C&P contacted CrossCheck and, on its recommendation, accepted the check. When the check was dishonored, C&P mailed it to CrossCheck, which reimbursed C&P and sent a letter to Winterstein, requesting payment. Winterstein filed a suit in a federal district court against CrossCheck, asserting that the letter violated the Fair Debt Collection Practices Act. CrossCheck filed a motion for summary judgment. On what ground might the court grant the motion? Explain.

[*Winterstein v. CrossCheck, Inc.*, 149 F.Supp.2d 466 (N.D.Ill. 2001)]

After you have answered this problem, compare your answer with the sample answer given on the Web site that accompanies this text. Go to www.thomsonedu.com/westbuslaw/let, select "Chapter 17," and click on "Case Problem with Sample Answer."

17–6. Fair Credit Reporting Act. Source One Associates, Inc., is based in Poughquag, New York. Peter Easton, Source One's president, is responsible for its daily operations. Between 1995 and 1997, Source One received requests from persons in Massachusetts seeking financial information about individuals and businesses. To obtain this information, Easton first obtained the targeted individuals' credit reports through Equifax Consumer Information Services by claiming the reports would be used only in connection with credit transactions involving the consumers. From the reports, Easton identified financial institutions at which the targeted individuals held accounts and then called the institutions to learn the account balances by impersonating either officers of the institutions or the account holders. The information was then provided to Source One's customers for a fee. Easton did not know why the customers wanted the information. The state ("Commonwealth") of Massachusetts filed a suit in a Massachusetts state court against Source One and Easton, alleging, among other things, violations of the Fair Credit Reporting Act (FCRA). Did the defendants violate the FCRA? Explain. [*Commonwealth v. Source One Associates, Inc.*, 436 Mass. 118, 763 N.E.2d 42 (2002)]

17–7. Deceptive Advertising. "Set up & Ready to Make Money in Minutes Guaranteed!" the ads claimed. "The Internet Treasure Chest (ITC) will give you everything you need to start your own exciting Internet business including your own worldwide website all for the unbelievable price of only $59.95." The ITC "contains virtually everything you need to quickly and easily get your very own worldwide Internet business up, running, stocked with products, able to accept credit cards and ready to take orders almost immediately." What ITC's marketers—Damien Zamora and end70 Corp.—did not disclose were the significant additional costs required to operate the business: domain name registration fees, monthly Internet access and hosting charges, monthly fees to access the ITC product warehouse, and other "upgrades." The Federal Trade Commission filed a suit in a federal district court against end70 and Zamora, seeking an injunction and other relief. Are the defendants' claims "deceptive advertising"? If so, what might the court order the defendants to do to correct any misrepresentations? [*Federal Trade Commission v. end70 Corp.*, __F.Supp.2d__ (N.D.Tex. 2003)]

17–8. Debt Collection. 55th Management Corp. in New York City owns residential property that it leases to various tenants. In June 2000, claiming that one of the tenants, Leslie Goldman, owed more than $13,000 in back rent, 55th

Once, in a cornfield in Mexico, there lived a little red ant. She shared an anthill with her nine hundred ninety-nine cousins. They looked exactly alike except for the little red ant. She was a bit smaller than the others.

Early one fall morning all the ants crawled from their anthill. They paraded single file across the field, looking for food to store for the winter. Because her legs were shorter, the little red ant was last in line.

"¡Amigos!" she called. "Wait for me."

"Quick!" scolded the others. "¡Pronto!"

The larger ants began to return to the nest, carrying scraps of corn on top of their heads. They left nothing behind for the little red ant. Then she spied something yellow under a leaf. It was the color of corn, but it smelled much sweeter.

The ant guessed at once what it was.

"¡Torta!" exclaimed the little red ant.

Perhaps a bird had dropped the cake from the sky. Perhaps a mouse had dug it from the ground. But now this wonderful crumb of cake belonged to her.

"Lucky me!" said the little red ant.

She tired to push the crumb. "Oooof!" she puffed.

She tried to pull it. "Ugh!" she panted.

She sighed and said, "I need someone strong to carry my crumb for me."

The little red ant covered the cake with the leaf again. Then she set off down the row of cornstalks to find someone strong to help her.

The ant had not gone far when she spied a log.

"A log is nice for resting," she said, climbing up on it.

"Get off!"

The ant jumped down. She discovered a pointy nose at one end of the log. At the other end she found a twitching tail.

The ant guessed at once what it was.

"¡El Lagarto!" exclaimed the little red ant.

"Buenos días," the ant said politely to the lizard. "Good morning. I am looking for someone strong."

El Lagarto puffed his cheeks. "I'm so strong I can blow down an anthill!"

"Not that!" the ant cried. "I want you to carry my big crumb of cake."

"Too cold," grumbled the lizard. "I'm stiff as a stick until El Sol warms me up."

"Then El Sol is stronger than you are," said the ant. "I shall ask the sun to help me."

"We can wait for him together," El Lagarto whispered. He flicked out his long tongue. "Come closer."

"No, gracias," the ant said quickly. "No, thank you!" She did not want to be breakfast for a hungry lizard.

The little red ant ran down the row as fast as her six legs would take her.

She had not gone very far when she spied a cobweb stretched between two cornstalks. Shining through the web was the sun.

"Lucky me!" cried the ant. "There is El Sol—caught in a net!" She scrambled up the stalk.

"Stop shaking my ladder!"

The little red ant spied something black and yellow skipping across the web.

The ant guessed at once what it was.

"¡La Araña!" exclaimed the little red ant.

"Perdón," said the ant to the spider. "Excuse me. I am climbing to the sun to ask him to carry my crumb of cake. El Sol is very strong."

"Foolish ant!" scoffed the spider. "No one can climb so high. Anyhow, I know someone stronger than El Sol."

"Who?" asked the ant.

"El Gallo! He wakes the sun every morning."

16

"Then I shall ask him to help me," the ant declared.

"Stay a while," La Araña coaxed, "and keep me company."

The little red ant gazed up at the spider. The sun had moved higher in the sky and no longer seemed caught in the web. A fly was caught instead.

"No, gracias," said the ant quickly. She did not want La Araña to tie her up like the fly. "No, thank you."

The little red ant backed down the stalk and hurried on her way. She had not gone very far when she stumbled over the roots of two tall thin trees.

"¿Qué pasa?" a scratchy voice demanded. "What's happening?"

The ant rubbed her eyes. She saw that the roots were really claws. She saw that the trees were really legs. She looked up and saw a fierce face with beady eyes bending over her. A yellow beak snapped open and shut, and a red topknot bobbed up and down.

The ant guessed at once what it was.

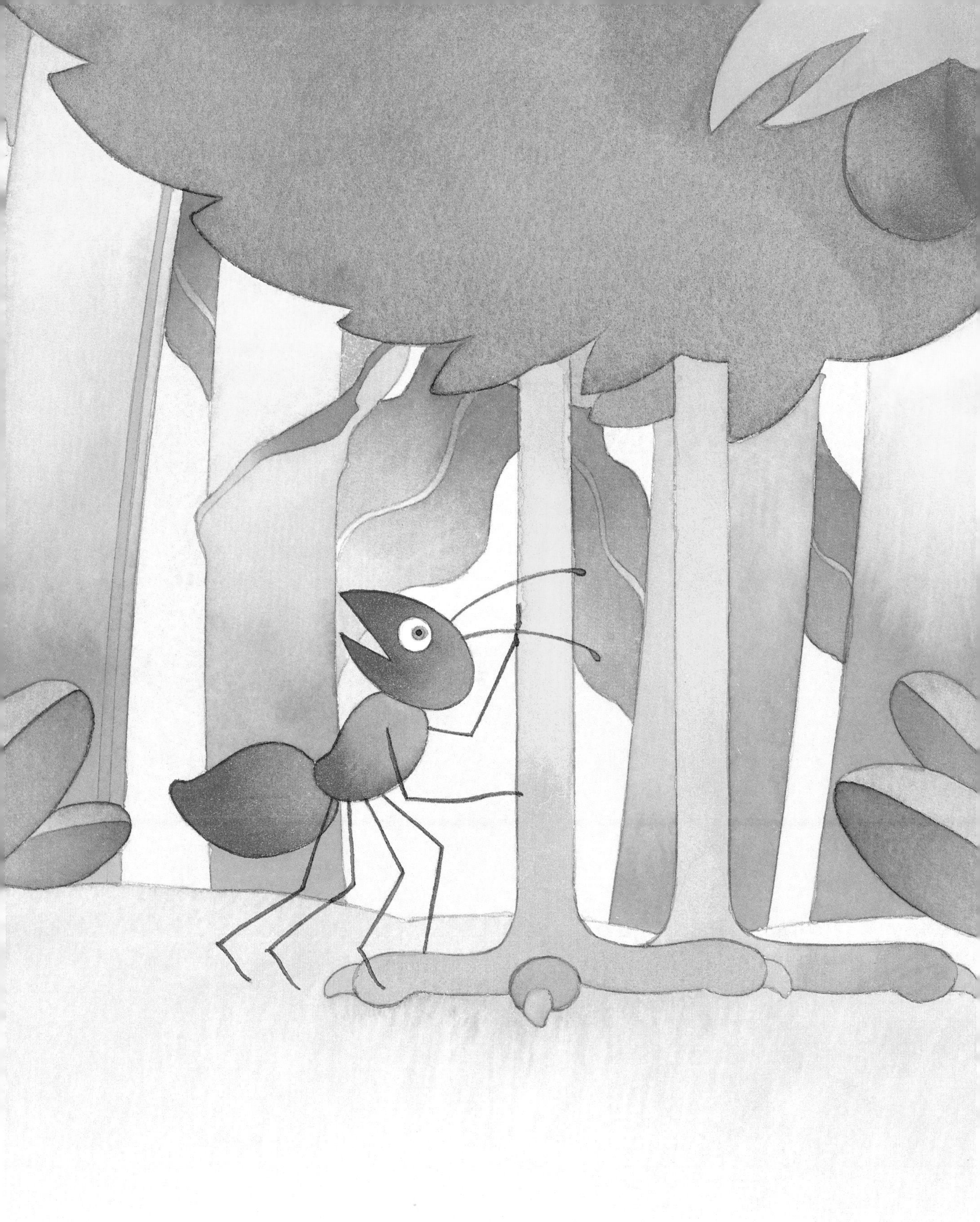

"¡El Gallo!" exclaimed the little red ant.

"Por favor . . ." the ant begged the rooster.
"Please . . . don't eat me!"

"Ants taste HORRIBLE!" squawked El Gallo.

"Then will you carry my crumb of cake for me?"

"I'm too busy." The rooster cocked his head.
"Did you say cake?"

"Sí," said the little red ant. "Yes."

"Cake tastes DELICIOUS!" crowed El Gallo.
"I shall eat your crumb myself!"

"But . . ." the ant began.

"Where is it?" The rooster ran about in circles.
"Awk!" he screeched suddenly. "Listen!"

"To what?" asked the ant.

"To that dreadful noise! It's the chicken-chaser!
Awk!" Flapping his wings, the rooster flew up and
over the cornstalks.

The ant was glad to see El Gallo go before he found her great big crumb. "Lucky me," said the little red ant, and hurried on her way.

She had not gone very far when she came upon something big and bristly. Its nose was pointed to the sky, and the dreadful noise was coming from its mouth.

The ant guessed at once what it was.

"¡El Coyote!" exclaimed the little red ant.

"¡Hola!" the ant shouted to the coyote. "Hello!"

El Coyote stopped in the middle of a howl and stared down his nose at the ant. "Don't bother me. I'm singing the sun a bedtime song." The coyote threw back his head, ready to howl again.

"You must be strong to sing so loudly," said the ant. "Will you carry my big crumb of cake for me?"

"Not now," said El Coyote. "Maybe tomorrow.
Or next week."

"But that might be too late!"

Suddenly the coyote pricked up his ears, and the
hair on his back stood on end. "¡Mira!" he yelped.
"Look! It is the terrible Hombre!" El Coyote tucked
his tail between his legs and dashed off through
the cornstalks.

The little red ant was sad to see him go. Then she
shrugged and started on her way again. But . . .

Something was moving down the row toward her.
It wore boots on its feet and a straw hat on its head.

The ant guessed at once what it was.

"¡El Hombre!" exclaimed the little red ant.

From far away, the man looked too small to help even an ant. But the nearer he came, the larger he got. Soon he was taller than the cornstalks, and his shadow stretched halfway down the row. He grew so tall that the little red ant could not even see the top of his hat.

"¡Señor!" called the ant. "Please carry my cake for me."

The man did not hear her. He kept walking.

Now the little red ant looked up and saw something terrifying. The heel of his huge boot hung over her head.

"¡Alto!" exclaimed the little red ant. "Stop!"

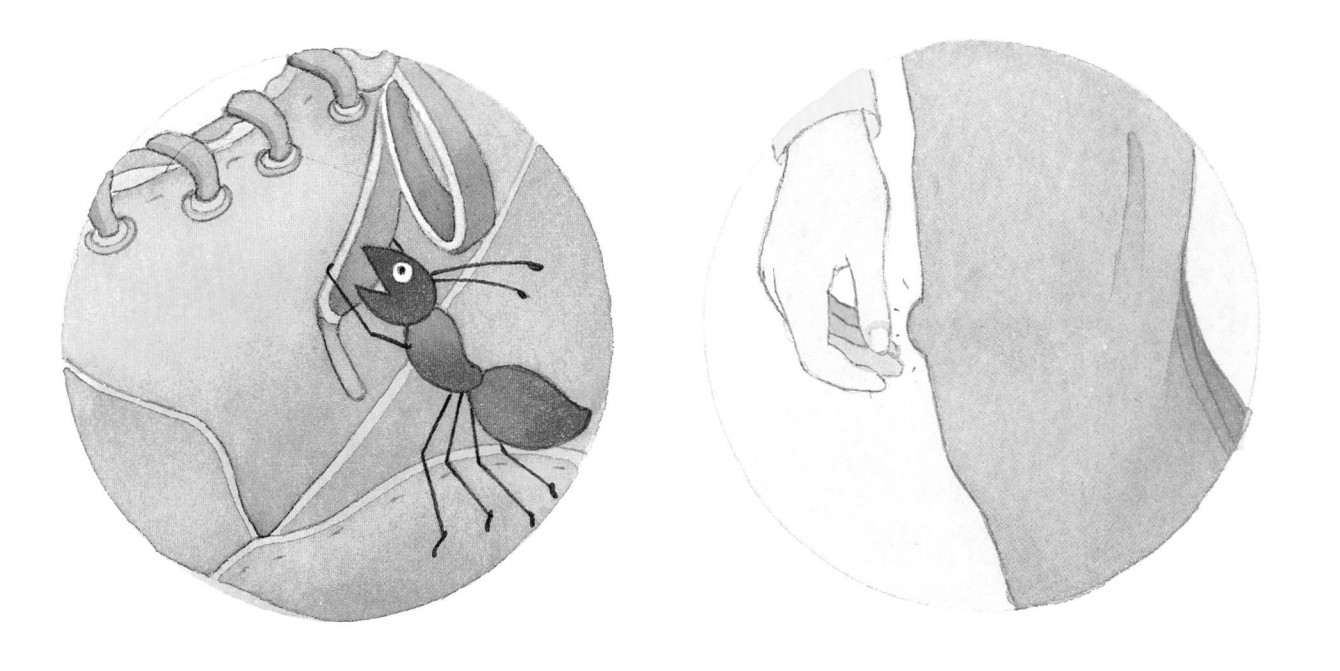

The man did not hear her. He kept walking. So . . .

The little red ant took a skip and a hop and caught hold of his shoelace. Then she ran up his leg.

The man rubbed his knee. So . . .

The little red ant scurried under his shirt.

The man scratched his chest. So . . .

29

The little red ant skittered over his shoulders.
The man slapped his neck. So . . .
The little red ant crept into his ear.
She shouted in her very loudest voice, "HELP ME!"

"Yi!" yelled the man. "Ticklebugs!" He shook his head and jumped up and down.

The straw hat flew from his head, and the little red ant tumbled down on top of it.

The man ran across the cornfield, still shouting, "TICKLEBUGS!"

The ant watched him go. "Adiós, señor," she called. "Goodbye." Then she thought of something quite surprising.

"I frighten El Hombre . . . who scares El Coyote . . . who chases El Gallo . . . who wakes El Sol . . . who warms El Lagarto . . . who can blow down an anthill. So . . .

"I AM THE STRONGEST OF ALL!"

The little red ant crawled off the hat. She followed her trail back through the cornstalks, just the way she had come. At last she reached her crumb of cake and pulled off the leaf.

"Aah," said the ant, sniffing. The cake was warm and sticky and smelled sweeter than ever.

She took a big, big breath. Then, ever so slowly, she lifted the crumb. She lifted it up and up until she could put it on top of her head. Then . . .

Step by step,
inch by inch,
all by herself,
by the light of the moon,
the ant carried her wonderful cake home
to the anthill.
   She feasted on the crumb all winter long.
And, when springtime came . . .

she was exactly the same size as her cousins.
"Lucky me!" exclaimed La Hormiga, the ant.

Author's Note

The fable about a persistent little ant has been told for centuries in Europe. A number of different versions are found in France, Portugal, and Spain. The ant's specific quest for help changes from place to place, as do the characters she encounters. Although this variation is based on a Spanish tale, it has taken on a distinctly Mexican flavor.

Like all fables, this one has a moral. Wherever and however the story is told, the ant always carries this message:

You can do it if you think you can.

Characters

El Lagarto	el lahGAHRtoh	The Lizard
El Sol	el SOHL	The Sun
La Araña	lah ahRAHnyah	The Spider
El Gallo	el GAHyoh	The Rooster
El Coyote	el cohYOHtay	The Coyote
El Hombre	el OHMbray	The Man
La Hormiga	lah ohrMEEgah	The Ant

Other Spanish Words

Amigos	ahMEEgohss	Friends
¡Pronto!	PROHNtoh	Quick!
Torta	TOHRtah	Cake
Sí	SEE	Yes
Buenos días	BWAYnohss DEEahss	Good morning
Gracias	GRAHsyahss	Thank you
Perdón	payrDOHN	Excuse me
¿Qué pasa?	KAY PAHsah	What's happening?
Por favor	POHR fahVOHR	Please
¡Mira!	MEErah	Look!
Señor	SAYnyohr	Mister
¡Alto!	AHLtoh	Stop!
Adiós	ahDYOHSS	Goodbye